Poe was an exceptional pilot who fought with the Resistance against the vicious First Order. The First Order was intent on taking over the galaxy.

General Leia, the leader of the Resistance, recruited Poe for a special mission. She needed to track down her long lost brother, Luke Skywalker, who was a powerful Jedi.

In order to find Luke, Poe and his whirring, beeping

droid, BB-8, needed to first track down a man called

Lor San Tekka. Would he know where the last Jedi was?

However, the First Order's terrifying commanders, Captain Phasma and Kylo Ren, had also been sent to find Lor San Tekka. They had heard rumours that he possessed a map that could lead them to Luke. But one stormtrooper called FN-2187 did not want to go on this mission. He wondered if it was the right thing to do.

Lor San Tekka lived on a distant desert

planet called Jakku and it was there that

Poe and BB-8 flew.

Unknown to the two freedom fighters, First

Order ships were also flying there.

After searching the isolated planet, Poe eventually found Lor San Tekka. The old man gave Poe a map which would help Leia find Luke.

Luke had once been a great Jedi Knight, who could control the Force. The Force was an energy field that could be used for good or bad. Luke was now in hiding.

Meanwhile, the First Order troopers were also

landing on Jakku.

They began searching for Lor San Tekka.

When he realised the troopers were there, Poe gave

the mysterious map to BB-8, who whizzed away into

the desert. If the map was found by the First Order

all hope would be lost!

The stormtroopers began to hurt the people on Jakku, desperately trying to force information from them. Someone had to know where the map was! FN-2187 refused to harm anyone.

The troopers eventually captured Poe and took him

to Kylo Ren.

The evil commander wanted the map and was

furious when he learned that Poe no longer had it.

If only he could find Luke first and defeat him!

The First Order troopers dragged Poe back to
their ship.

Poe was locked in a dark, lonely prison cell.

Captain Phasma was outraged by FN-2187's

behaviour on Jakku as he had not followed her

orders. She demanded to see him immediately.

Meanwhile, back in the prison cell, Kylo Ren used the Force to make Poe tell him where the map was hidden. Poe reluctantly told him that BB-8 had it.

FN-2187 had made a decision. He no longer wanted to be part of the First Order and its cruel regime. But FN-2187 needed help if he was to escape.

FN-2187 crept stealthily into the prison cell and freed Poe. They would escape the First Order as a team! All they needed now was a ship!

Together, the two men stole a TIE fighter as the troopers blasted deadly lasers at them.

As they soared away, the First Order ship fired

on their TIE fighter!

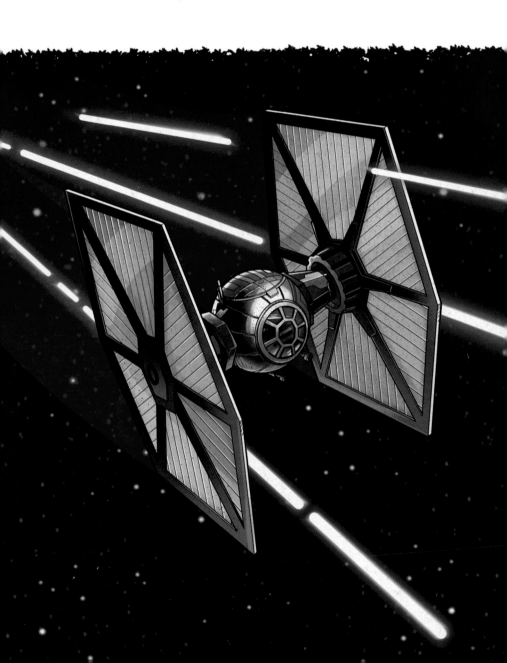

Poe flew the TIE fighter, with the help of his new
co-pilot.

By twisting and turning and swooping and wheeling through space, they managed to escape the First Order.

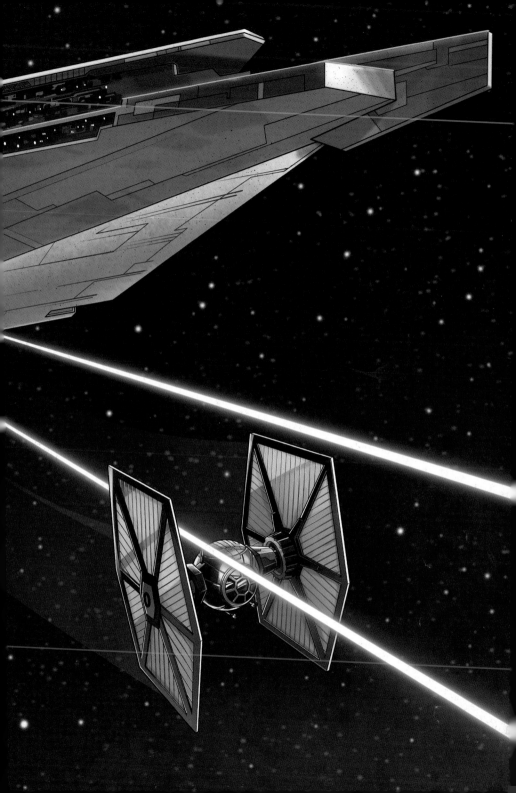

Poe looked at his new friend and FN-2187 smiled back.

'My name is FN-2187,' he said shyly.

'Then I shall call you Finn!' Poe laughed.

But now they needed to find BB-8 and locate the map that would lead them to Luke. Could this Jedi Knight really help them in their battle against the First Order?

As they raced to their next mission, Poe felt proud of Finn. They made a great team and were now ready for their next mission!